... To Emma ....

Dare to Dream - Dream to Dare

...And... to Pick Your (Knows?) —

Always remember

Carole Hamburger

The Zippity-Do-Dot
The Dot Who Dared to Pick Her Knows

Written & Illustrated By
Carole Hamburger

*Best Always
Carole Hamburger*

CHERRY STREET PRESS
Philadelphia, PA

To Carl....for all the right reasons

Life is either a daring adventure...
Or it is nothing at all...

Helen Keller

The future belongs to
Those who believe in their dreams...

Eleanor Roosevelt

Go confidently in the direction of your dreams...
Live the life you have imagined...

Henry David Thoreau

First Edition-First Printing 2008
ISBN: 978-0-9764921-1-5
Library of Congress: 2007906838
Copyright © 2008 by Carole Hamburger
Printed and bound in Singapore

A long time ago in The Dot Family

There was Mama and Papa – and baby made three.

Their first child, a Star-Pupil, had brought them such joy.

So they hoped for a second…a girl or a boy.

And since they lived in the City of Sibling-Affection

With signs of it pointing from every direction –

It seemed only natural to now have another.

They'd love a new baby – and so would Big Brother!

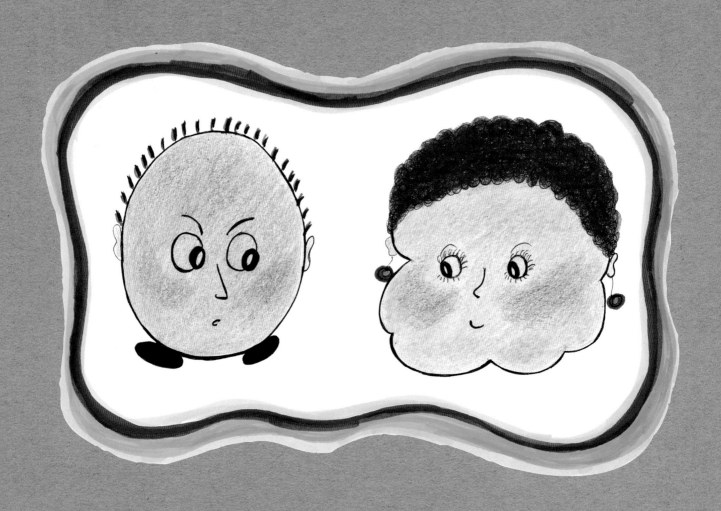

In time Mama-Dot became moody and grumpy
And Papa-Dot thought that she looked slightly lumpy.
She seemed to be bigger with each passing day –
And walked with a waddle in such a strange way!
And she constantly craved ice cream, pickles, and chips…
Until the day came both her feet were eclipsed!
These symptoms detected, they strongly suspected
A new dot-addition would soon be expected.

Sure enough! Doctor-Dot gave confirmation.
A wee-one was coming – he had information
That this was a daughter – due end of December.
But she arrived sooner…the Ninth of September!
When she entered the world with a hoot and a holler
There wasn't one thing that could stop her or stall her.
This early debut was the first clue their tot
Would be quick – a self-starter – a dynamo dot!

Being a preemie she was so petite.

A diminutive dot – but her parts were complete.

She was checked all around – front, back, and her sides…

And found to be perfect in spite of her size.

From her top to her bottom – her left to her right,

She was three-hundred-sixty degrees of delight!

Well-curved and well-balanced in every direction,

This child seemed the essence of daughter perfection.

But her folks didn't know – for she was just born,

That this was the 'calm before the storm'.

How could they know? She wasn't yet showing

The chaos she'd cause when she would start growing.

She slept like an angel, so snug in her bed,

So how could they know there'd be troubles ahead?

This miniscule miracle they had created
Left Mama and Papa so thrilled and elated
That Papa was walking-on-air…on Cloud Nine.
And Mama was tickled pink all of the time.
They showered their princess with so much affection
That she could feel love come from every direction.

She was watched like a hawk – never out of their sight.
Mama walked her all day – Papa rocked her all night.
Always rockabyed – lullabyed – pampered – and pacified –
Ever so satisfied – that's why she never cried.
But right round-the-bend there was 'bedlam a brewing'.
They just couldn't tell cause she wasn't yet *doing*.
She gave not one inkling of what was to come –
So how could her folks know they'd soon 'come undone'?

Never were two parents ever so smitten!
She was their *lambchop* – their *cupcake* – their *kitten*.
Each pet-name they called her got cuter and cuter.
But when she got older would these cute names suit her?
She needed a *real* name to call all her own –
A name for right now and for when she was grown.
So Papa climbed down from Cloud Nine just in time
To help Mama find her a name that fit fine.

They first thought of Dottie...but Dottie-the-Dot
Sounded silly – *redundant* – so certainly *not!*
Then they went through the alphabet without delay
Sorting out names in an orderly way.
They tried Annabelle – Brandy – Carlotta – and Dolly –
Emmylou – Franny – Gianna – and Holly.
When they reached letter 'I' they knew that was *it.*
They picked **Isadora** – the most perfect fit!
And in a pinch she'd have two dandy nick names
Because *Iz* and *Izzy* could be handy quick names.

7

In the hospital Izzy was sugar and spice.
So cuddly and snuggly – so sweet and so nice.
On her first day at home she was docile and quiet –
But by the *next* day she was causing a riot!
On the second day home, from pre-dawn till past dusk,
She rumbled – and tumbled – and tantrumed – and fussed.
Just a single day older, but with increased vigor,
She got a bit bolder and grew a bit bigger.
The house was chaotic – the calm was disrupted.
On Day 'Two' at home her demeanor erupted!
Her folks found that naming her proved to be easy
Compared to now taming her – that left them queasy…
And overwhelmed, overworked, worn out, and weary.
They just weren't prepared for their pepper-pot deary.
Izzy's *'Terrible Twos'* had arrived oh so quickly!
The Dots were beside themselves – feeling quite sickly.

Now each passing day brought a brand new surprise.
Oh! The things Izzy did right before her folk's eyes.
For though she was small...just barely an ouncer,
She quickly rolled over, became quite a bouncer.
Then a bumper – a jumper – a rocker – a roller.
Try as they might they just couldn't control her.
Soon a flipper – a skipper – a flopper – a hopper.
Nothing would calm her and no-one could stop her.
She stayed in a state of perpetual motion…
Her antics were wild, causing such a commotion!
Izzy seemed to have schemes that were planned out and plotted,
Causing more grief than one dot was allotted.
To call her 'precocious' was truly an error.
This child was 'atrocious' – a total *dot-terror!*
Since Izzy was stuck in her '*Terrible Twos*',
Poor Mama and Papa now both had the blues!

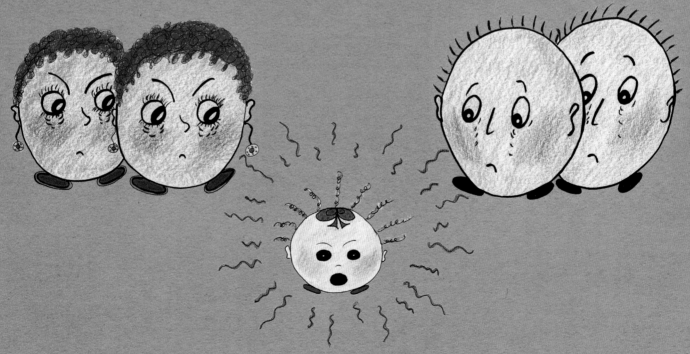

As time tumbled by Iz became *more* defiant.
All twenty-four-seven she stayed noncompliant.
Rollicking, frolicking, through night and day
With 'Whys?' and 'Why-Nots?' that would not go away.
And whatever was said by her father and mother
Went *right in* one ear…and then *left out* the other!

Clearly, both of her folks were distraught and dismayed
By the wild stubborn-streak Isadora displayed.
Late every night she would jump out of bed…
Turn cartwheels – do backflips – and stand on her head.

When she zoomed round the room
Like a turbo-charged twister,
Her well behaved brother
Steered clear of his sister!

Now more than a handful, this out-of-hand daughter
Made both her folks chase her – but they rarely caught her.
When she started racing…outpacing her folks,
She ran circles round them – they thought they'd have strokes!

At first The Dots thought that their difficult daughter
Would benefit from all the lessons they taught her.
They plied and cajoled her with treats and diversions,
Then tried to withhold extra sweets and excursions.
But all of their efforts were futile – for naught.
Their renegade daughter refused to be taught!
She remained rowdy, and surly, and sassy.
They just couldn't harness their live-wired lassie.
And as time took its toll Isadora grew **bolder!**
Finally her folks said, "NO MORE!" – then they told her…

But when they said 'NO MORE!'– she heard '**KNOW**' more!
She was feisty and fearless – more so than before.
Her tongue and her feet just got louder and faster.
The problem grew bigger – it was a disaster!
When told to behave, she would sulk and then pout,
Spouting 'Whys?' and 'Why-Nots?' that were spoken in **SHOUT!**
So both Mama and Papa stayed blue as she battled…
But not Isadora – she *never* got rattled.
Miss Iz, 'Queen of Chaos', caused her folks such trouble –
Still blue and beside themselves – now they saw *double!!*

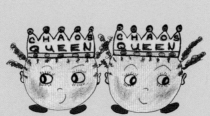
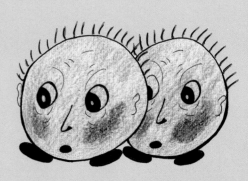

Izzy's behavior became so alarming!

It wasn't becoming – it sure wasn't charming.

Her folks needed rest, and they needed it fast.

Izzy's wild childhood days would be put in the past.

It was now time for smiles and some over-due happiness.

Time to rid Iz of her over-ripe sassiness.

But her folks couldn't tame her – and they both knew it.

They needed assistance to help them get through it.

So without hesitation The Dots both agreed

To find the best coach who could channel her speed.

When they finally found Tumble-Tots, chock full of drills,

They planned to relax while Iz practiced new skills.

Next day, bright and early, they got Iz enrolled
And hoped that the Tot-Coach could get her controlled.
The class seemed like Play Day, which really pleased Izzy.
Coach taught her to listen and kept her so busy.
Each day he would say, "Give it all that you've got!"
Cause Coach knew the power of positive thought.
He seldom said 'Stop!'– and he scarcely said 'No!'
Instead he said, "Know what you're doing, then Go!"
So she danced on the mat with her feet toe-to-heel.
Did somersaults, handstands, and cartwheels with zeal.
Then she pranced on the balance beam – flipped on the bars –
While Coach told her daily to *Reach for the Stars!*
Every day Izzy tackled new 'Knows' in her drills,
Then practiced till perfect, perfecting new skills.
Yes, Iz took to Tot-Class like bees take to honey.
Soon her disposition got sweeter and sunny.
The Tumble-Tot classes made Izzy *so* happy!
Her Mama got giddy – and so did her Pappy!

On the last day of Tot-Class Coach Cranch told The Dots
That he was so pleased – he shared so many thoughts…

Your Isadora has natural ability. She moves through her paces with grace and agility. Whatever the task, whatever I ask her - She learns it fast! No-one has surpassed her! She runs like the wind - Jumps like a gazelle. There isn't a thing Izzy doesn't do well. With her round-stable body and sound-able mind, your Izzy is truly a ONE-OF-A-KIND! And as her Coach I can honestly say…Isadora's 'well-rounded in EVERY way!

Gosh! I'm elated! I can see why Coach is so Top-Rated!

Wow! I never anticipated that our troubles would be so quickly abated!

The Dots were amazed and quite frankly astonished.
Their Iz was a Tot-Star...and never admonished!
The class had worked wonders – the change was dramatic.
Both Mama and Papa were simply ecstatic!
Now they saw the light and they well understood
That Izzy was trying as hard as she could…
Cause as Tumble-Tot classes came to a close
Little Izzy was tamed from her *head* to her *toes*.
Yes, their 'hard-boiled' daughter had done a 'one-eighty'
To *sunny-side-up*…she'd became a young lady!

No longer a rebel with cause, spunky Izzy
Was happy and free because she was kept busy.
Long-gone were the days when she acted so wild…
She transformed to a more mellow, well mannered child.
And since all the fussing had upped and abated
Both Mama and Papa were truly elated!
Now that their Izzy was trying her best,
The Dots got some rest and were no longer stressed.
Their life became tranquil – quite calm and serene…
The whole family got back to a happy routine.
And though Tot-Class had ended, as all good things must,
On her first day of school Iz was glad to be bused.

Excited and eager – and ready to learn,
Izzy rushed to her class – that's when she met **Miss Stern!**
Her teacher, Miss Stern, said…

So Izzy sat down and thought…

But Izzy knew better because she was tamed.
She stayed in her seat – didn't want to be shamed.
So she stared out the window and gazed at the sky –
Then longed for the playground and agonized why
She couldn't play in the yard with her peers,
Skipping and flipping – and shifting her gears.
When Miss Stern caught her daydreaming she promptly said…

Izzy complied and tried hard to obey.
She stopped all her daydreaming during the day.
Then her eyes roamed the room till she spotted a chart –
A chart Miss Stern posted to make the class smart.
When Iz saw the handwriting up on the wall
She thought…

16

Poor Isadora! Upset from the start.
Stuck in her chair and she disliked that chart!
Miss Stern's list of rules was a constant reminder
Of action packed days, full of fun, far behind her.
But still, Isadora tried *so* hard to please.
She stayed just as quiet as those silent 'E's.

On the first day of testing Iz proved to Miss Stern
That there wasn't much that she still had to learn.
She was first in the class to tie both her shoes –
To polish her 'P's and perfect all her 'Q's.
She dotted each 'i' – crossed all 'f's and 't's.
Said 'Please' – 'Thanks' – and 'Bless You' if anyone sneezed.
She learned to count quickly by twos, fives, and tens.
Reported with Who, What, Why, Where – even Whens.
Became a speed reader with full comprehension,
Remembering each lesson with total retention.
Yes, Iz was advanced, past all others her age.
Speed reading aside, they weren't *on the same page!*
Every day Iz proved that she was a 'Knower'…
Unlike her classmates – some lazy – all slower!

It seemed all Miss Stern's students were lacking direction –
All except Izzy – she was the exception!
The others in class were a boisterous bunch
Who did their best *work* in the gym and at lunch!
Sabrina and Bobby were stuck-up and snobby.
Gussie was fussy – she needed a hobby.
Billy would dilly and Sally would dally.
Jervis was nervous – *especially* near Sally.
Sometimes Steven was even – at other times odd.
The most level-headed were Milton and Maude.
Twins Horace and Morris caused *everyone* trouble.
When they got detention Miss Stern gave them double!
And the class clown-around was a prankster named Chester
Who pestered Miss Stern and was always sequestered.

Slim Tim was unbalanced – he leaned upon Sue.

But Sue leaned on *him*…she was unbalanced too!

And Seymour was spiraling out of control.

He guessed on all tests – he was stressed – the poor soul!

A cute little cookie named Ginger was snappy.

She tormented Seymour, who *never* was happy.

Jack and Jill copied off their neighbor Flo –

Until they found out that her grades were so low!

Mary and Maisy were nasty and lazy.

They bickered and snickered and drove Miss Stern crazy.

Emma was testy, contrite, and contrary.

What a dilemma! She sat next to Mary.

And Johnny-Come-Lately was constantly tardy.

Miss Stern knew that *Izzy* was her only smarty!

When others got stumped or got stuck in their tracks
It was Izzy who jumped up with all of the facts.
In rapid succession, not missing a beat,
She rattled her 'Knows' off then sat in her seat.
But none of her classmates were passing a test!
Miss Stern was concerned and said…

When Iz heard those words she thought…

In that instant she had an idea for a chart
With a list of school rules sure to make the class smart.
She wanted to start on her chart right away
But wondered if Miss Stern would give the okay –
Or would she say 'No!' with a grunt and a groan?
Iz knew she should wait for advice back at home…
Where Mama and Papa could guide and advise her
Because they were older and they were both wiser.

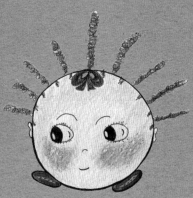

Papa said, "Iz, if you think that you're right,
Start on your chart – you can do it tonight.
It's not *what* you say, but *how* you deliver –
So mention Miss Stern and make sure that you give her
Ideas that will help her to make the class smart.
Ideas that come both from your head and your heart.
If you don't *break* the rules, only *bend* them a bit,
Miss Stern might admit that your chart's a good fit.
Even dots can move mountains – believe me, it's true!
So go for it Izzy…it's now up to you."

Mama said, "Izzy, whatever you do,
Use words that inspire and matter to you.
The words that we use are such powerful tools,
So choose them with care when you write your school rules.
And since all of life is a balancing act,
Kindly mention Miss Stern and be sure to use tact.
Just don't ruffle her feathers or step on her toes
Because you and Miss Stern must be friends – never foes.
With all said, if you're sure this is what you must do –
Sleep on it tonight…you might get a clear view."

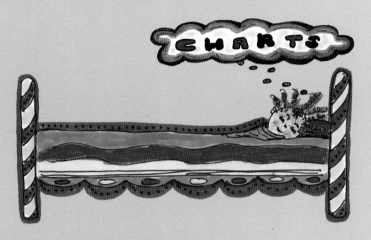

That night Izzy gingerly jumped into bed
With visions of charts whizzing inside her head.
She dreamt of her chart till the dawn shed its light –
Designing – refining – made each word just right.
And she prudently heeded her parent's advice
By pleasing Miss Stern…Izzy mentioned her *twice!*
The whole thing had magically popped in her head.
Miss Stern had been right – dreams *were* better in bed!
That morning she wrote out her chart in a jiffy
In bold red and black – it looked smart – it looked spiffy.
Then she took it to class and with caution displayed it,
And to her delight Miss Stern more than OK'd it.
Miss Stern read it aloud then she clearly announced…

Class, my old list of rules is officially trounced! We now have a new chart created by Izzy. I think it's fantastic…. and if you get busy learning your lessons and trying real hard, I promise to let you play out in the yard!

In-KNOW-Sent
Rules for School Success

Know how to laugh – know how to smile
Know how to talk to a friend for a while
Know how to stand straight and look folks in the eye
Know how to speak up and give new things a try
Know how to ask for help if you need it
Know how to love a good book when you read it
Know how to listen – know how to study
Know how to offer some help to your buddy
Know when to hurry – know when to wait
Know how to be kind and co-operate
Know how to say Please-Thank-You-Sorry and Pardon
Know how to stop and smell flowers in the garden
Know how to make friends and how to belong
Know there's a difference between right and wrong
Know how to be kind to all living creatures
Know how to please your folks and your teachers

• • • • •

Know if we all start working real hard
Miss Stern will allow us to play in the yard
Know that Miss Stern wants us all to be smart
Let's show her we're trying and make a new start!

23

Miss Stern loved the 'Know' chart – that was a no-brainer.
The class got inspired – the climate got saner.
Now they all tried to ace every pop-quiz and test
And felt pleased-as-punch to be doing their best.
When Miss Stern sang their praises in major and minor
She told them…

No class in the world could be finer! Your grades and behavior are TOPS-you've worked hard- You've earned DOUBLE RECESS and PLAY in the YARD!

Then Miss Stern turned to Izzy and said with a smile…

You're a scholarly dot. I've known that for a while. Your chart is the best... and I sense you are bored...For both of these reasons you're due a REWARD!

I'm due a reward? What will it be? So many good things are happening to me! I dreamt of a chart, and made it come true..... I dreamt of more playtime and that happened too! If I have more dreams that matter to me, will they become a reality?

24

What a sensation this new chart was!

News of it spread – the whole school was abuzz!

And now that the class had all buckled down,

Word of their progress spread throughout the town.

When a May Day Assembly was called by the teachers,

They met in the gym and sat up in the bleachers.

Miss Stern was awarded the Best-Teacher trophy!

(That's how the class learned her first name was Sophie.)

She was named...'Teacher-of-the-Year'...

And gladly accepted, but then made it clear

That the reason her class was the *best* in the nation –

Done with hard work and with no grade inflation –

Was due to the 'Know' chart created by Izzy.

That was the reason her class got so busy!

Then Miss Stern turned to Izzy and said with pride…

Isadora, soon you will be taking a ride...
You've proven you're quick and surely a 'Do-er.'
You're a **Zippity-Do-Dot!** Nothing could be
truer! Now you need to be stretched with more
advanced knowledge. It's time for new 'Knows.'
You can pick them in **College!** So with pleasure I
grant you this 'Top-Dot' Award! It's your
own Scholar-Ship with Free-Ticket to board.
Your ship goes to **HARVARD.** It's stamped on the
card. I'm sure you'll be Happy inside Harvard-Yard!

Miss Stern knew the schoolyard
Was Izzy's first pleasure –
So she chose her a school
With a Yard beyond measure.
Izzy was gleeful!
She *loved* Miss Stern's choice.
Then she spoke to the group
In her most grateful voice…

A million 'Thank-Yous' could not be enough!
I'll miss everyone – it will really be **tough**
To say 'Goodbye' and be on my way –
But the ticket is **dated** – it says **LEAVE TODAY!**

Scholar-Ship Ride
Cost: **FREE TICKET**
Issued to: **ISADORA DOT**
Destination: **HARVARD**
Date: **LEAVE TODAY**

Izzy was given a ticket to ride
On her own Scholar-Ship set to leave at high tide.
Her parents escorted her down to the jetty.
They hugged her and kissed her and missed her already.
Yet they knew in their hearts that she needed to go –
There were so many new things she needed to know.

Then they gave Isadora some extra supplies
To use as she sailed underneath open skies.
A compass, a map, and a highlighter marker.
A flashlight for times when the blue skies grew darker.
An iPod, a whistle, some sunscreen, a hat.
A laptop, some water, a soft sleeping mat.
A toothbrush, some toothpaste, hair ribbons and bows.
An extra large notebook for writing new 'Knows'.
Assorted selections of sensible snacks.
And a pink puffy pillow so she could relax.
A journal, a pen, and a good book to read.
A fax, and perhaps the thing she'd mostly need…
A cell-phone to use so that she could call home
Whenever she wanted – wherever she'd roam.

Star-Pupil was fond of his little kid-sister
But he couldn't be there – was sad that he missed her.
Seems he wasn't able to share the enjoyment.
He was traveling the road seeking future employment.
However, he called on the phone, spoke for hours…
And sent Iz a beautiful bouquet of flowers.

Miss Stern arrived right after class and delivered
A cold weather sweater in case Izzy shivered.
She told her that she was already a 'star'…
And to gather more 'Knows' – they would take her *so far!*

Coach also followed her down to the ship.
He waved and he wished her a safe happy trip.
Then he gave her a watch from both him and his wife
Inscribed…'*Stay right on-track for the Time of Your Life*'.

FOLLOW YOUR DREAMS

It was hard seeing Izzy go off on her own –
Charting a course bound for places unknown.
But The Dots knew that Izzy would bloom like a rose
If they sent her with Love to this world of new 'Knows'.
And their gift, Pearls-of-Wisdom, were etched with a phrase
That Iz would remember for all of her days.

Izzy boarded her ship with her gifts and her gear
And planned for the trip with her usual flair.
She polished her rails and got the course charted,
Then hoisted her sails so the trip could get started.
Once giving her schooner a ship-shape inspection
She sped straight ahead in a Northern Direction –
Sailing with moonlight and North Star to guide her
While keeping her gifts and supplies safe beside her.
The wind and the waves gave the boat ample motion…
Some rocking – some rolling – afloat on the ocean.

As she drifted along under moonbeams and light
That lit up the sky on that Scholar-Ship Night,
She swiftly advanced as her rainbow sails billowed…
Lost in her thoughts – very comfy and pillowed.
When she rocked off to sleep dreams took hold and unfurled
Painting seasonal scenes – one was *out-of-this-world!*
What could this mean dreaming of the four seasons?
Iz woke up and wondered if she'd learn the reasons.

Just then Old Father Time appeared out of thin air!
It seems he could do that – anytime – anywhere.
As he spoke his voice carried the wisdom of ages
Gathered through Time from the prophets and sages.
"Isadora, I know you can't stand the suspense,
But some time in the future these dreams will make sense."

"Iz, I've been at your side from your very first day.
From your '*Terrible Twos*' to your Tumble-Tot play.
I was with you in school when your chart helped Miss Stern,
And I watched you get gifts – but now it's *my* turn.
So Isadora, to You from Me…
Is the 'Time of Your Life' – in a package of three."

"Box 'One' are your memories – your history.
And Box 'Three' is uncertain – a mystery.
But the time in Box 'Two' is your *here* and your *now*…
Your time to Go-Do and make worthy of *Wow!*
And though each gift is valuable, Box Number 'Two'
Is the most precious present I'll ever give you.
Yes, Isadora, if truth be told…
It's worth more than all the world's silver and gold."
Then the Winds-of-Change quickly whisked him away
So that he could make time for the up-coming day.

Izzy's horizons were quickly expanding!
She docked the next day at the harborside landing.
Now finally in Boston – the home of Baked Beans,
The Red Sox, Tea Parties, Professors and Deans.
Hundreds of spectators gathered to greet her.
Even the mayor took time off to meet her!

Then the 'Welcome-to-College' Committee
Took her to Harvard Yard, west of the city.
Once there, she found *everyone picking their 'Knows'!*
And Izzy did too…Oh! The courses she chose.
Philosophy – Chemistry – Physics – and Voice.
Izzy *loved* picking! She loved every choice.
In class she was known as a *whiz* and a *scholar.*
Words seldom heard, but that's what the Profs called her…
So she sailed through her classes with effortless ease
And found time to play in The Yard when she pleased.

On long weekends she took time to chase her dreams, too,
By traveling to places to make them come true.

In fall Izzy hiked
Through the forest floor –
Exploring the canvas
Of colors galore!

In winter she skied from
Snow-capped peaks –
Zooming down trails
In zig-zagging streaks.

In summer she brought a beach ball and bucket
For frolic and fun on the Isle of Nantucket –
Where the sea met the sand – and the surf wet her toes.
The Life here was grand! What a way to get 'Knows'!

Now her seasonal dreams seemed to make perfect sense!
Almost all had come true – she had reached Future Tense.

Since each dream except *spring fling* in space had come true,
Izzy knew there was more that she needed to do.
So right after getting her Harvard Degree
She went down the road to MIT –
Where she was awarded a Ph.D.
In Astrophysics and Astronomy.

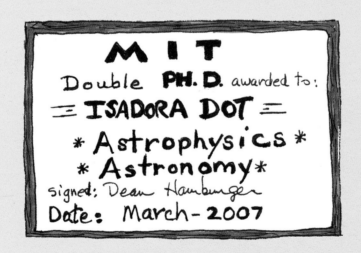

By March Izzy mastered all she'd been taught.
With her double-degree she was one *happy* dot!
Then when springtime marched forward from April to May –
Izzy officially got on her way…
On the Ninth day of May, in some far-away spot…
Isadora became the **World's First Astrodot!**

Now if you see a streak of bright light in the sky,
It's probably Izzy – whizzing on by.
Zooming about – out in cosmic space…
Having a *fling* with a smile on her face.
Doing just what she was meant to do…